ॐ

FANCY

of Dreams, Imagination & Flights of Fancy

Ashwini Kumar Aggarwal

जय गुरुदेव

ISBN13: 978-93-92201-28-8 Paperback Edition
ISBN13: 978-93-92201-36-3 Hardbound Edition
ISBN13: 978-93-92201-44-8 Digital Edition

Title: **Fancy**
Author: **Ashwini Kumar Aggarwal**

Printed and Published by
Devotees of Sri Sri Ravi Shankar Ashram
34 Sunny Enclave, Devigarh Road
Patiala 147001, Punjab, India

https://advaita56.weebly.com/
The Art of Living Centre

https://www.artofliving.org/

23rd December 2021 a happy fit Mummy expresses and her Soul brightens to enter the transcendental plane. 13th Poh Jor Mela Krishna Paksha Chaturthi, Pausha, Shishir Ritu, Ashlesha Nakshatra Vikram Samvat 2078 Ananda, Saka Era 1943 Plava

1st Edition December 2021

जय गुरुदेव

Dedication

Sri Sri Ravi Shankar

who keeps the Hope anything is possible

Blessing

All that you can do is to raise the level of Sattva. And then when Sattva's level is high, we have to wait one moment, any moment knowledge can dawn there.

All that you can do to have sunlight in this room, is to open the curtains and keep the windows open. And when dawn comes, it just dawns. You have the sunlight inside.

Sri Sri Ravi Shankar
A discourse on Yogasara Upanishad

Contents

Preface

Boys hope and achieve the impossible.

A single Soul can change the landscape and the fortunes of the entire planet.

Men may come and men may go, but the boyish Spirit remains alive and indomitable, nay incorrigible.

Prayer

शान्तिपाठः

ॐ स॒ह ना॑ववतु । स॒ह नौ भुनक्तु । स॒ह वी॒र्यं॑ करवावहै ।
ते॒ज॒स्वि ना॒वधी॑तमस्तु मा वि॑द्विषा॒वहै॑ ॥
ॐ शान्ति॒ः शान्ति॒ः शान्ति॑ः ॥

oṃ saha nāvavatu | saha nau bhunaktu | saha vīryaṃ karavāvahai
| tejasvi nāvadhītamastu mā vidviṣāvahai ||
oṃ śānti śānti śāntiḥ ||

Peace Invocation

O Pure Loving Grace!

May we be taken care of along with our family and friends.
May we enjoy socializing and eating together.
May we support each other's vision and growth.
May our intellect be open to new ideas and changing trends.
May we spend more time in praise than abuse, may we talk of each other's virtues rather than harp on vices.

Peace in our heart, in our body and in our environs.

1st Love

When the eyes open, there is sunshine and merriment.
Nature is blissful and peace abounds.

big guns

Big Guns Boom. Big Guns.

Thoughts t
U
M
B
L
e in a cascade

galaxies

galaxies chase each other.
A dance with friction shards n sparks
There ain't no one to spoil the show

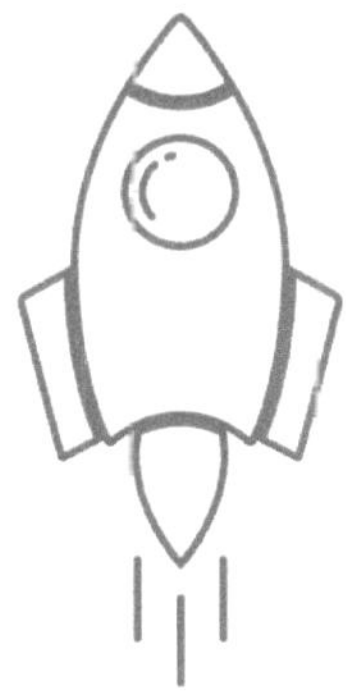

veld fox

A fox steps out of the veld. Seeing no one it runs gaily. Its body careening contouring evokes applause from the shrubs

someday

Someday I shall mingle with the Stars, play football with them, eat a bite off the Sun, and talk to the Blackhole.

once

Once I was a photon. I had Form.
Soon I became a phonon. I got a Name.

small bells and big drums
white conches and a brown flute
strings piano keys
brass and ivory
musical instruments shapely in looks
great to play saxophone violin guitar

me

Love flows in my veins,
Kindness flexes my muscles,
Patience colors my smile

.

Nobody knows it. None governs it. Naught comes close.
Yet they give it a name.

B R A H M A N

Big so big it cannot be grasped
Small so small there is a huge gap

end

Lands end we all know or have been.
Minds end is tough even for the docs,
Hearts End Is Far Beyond So Saints Too Don't Venture In

game

I played hockey as a child
And also dribbled a basketball

Somewhere along the way I found

Whatever kindled the WILL was a necessary game
That which spread SUNSHINE was the one true game

wonder

I used to wonder
WHY IS ME ME?
WHY ARE THEY THEY?

One day it struck
One a lake the other the moon
Both two sides of the same coin

boys

Boys grow brave and strong
They open up broad avenues
They make all taste abundance

hills

Hills loom large
Hills are mystical and grand
Hills are made up of solidified wishes
Where hills are densely shrubbed
Where hills have caves and openings
There the Lord visits frequently
There his aura is strongly evident

always sing and race up the road
race up the highway singing out loud
if you can run hard you shall win
victory is sweetest when hard won

tracks

I dream of moving tracks sans cars
weaving meandering crisscrossing
each street leads to home or work
both provide a cheery welcome

passengers

i made a square spaceship
it looked like a multicolored cube
its passages were made up of light
its crew was made up of sound

passengers boarded at will
some were from far off galaxies

<u>lo and behold</u>
suns also took a ride
blackholes also sat tight

i wondered whether to converse
with the handsome masculine Sun
or the beautiful feminine Blackhole?

The children had no such qualms
They chatted joyously and even ran out
of the square windows and toppled onto

the vast playgrounds of space

craft

i invented a craft that could
take me back in time
to glimpse my own birth
and even watch which part
of Me was mE

laser

my laser would travel to the moon and back
it brought back silver and shiny dust
it rode moonbeams
it waved at sunlight

girl

when the bells tinkle
when the ponytails whirl
when a continuous chatter is heard
know a girl is around,
know excitement abounds.

soul

deep inside the earth there is a soul
only few have noticed

it also hopes for
it also wishes
it also weeps and celebrates
it also chokes in gratefulness

time was my left hand
present was my right

sunrays were smiles
beauty my sight

M

medicine

I made a medicine
It healed illness within a couple of days

I made a massage
It cured the mind within the hour

What of cruelty or weakness?
Oh, that got erased in a trice.

Waves of music
Wafts of fragrance

))**^^((

Don’t give up

Will the Big
Hope the Best
Pray for the Element
Work hard to Match
Bring in genius Team
Lord is always at hand, within reach, and ready to assist

Not a penny
Not a quarter
But a whole vault full

redo

We shall fashion the fundamental laws
We shall reengineer gravity and electromagnetism
We shall redo the math in creation
We shall reenergize the constants like pi and light velocity

How soon can a city be built?
Just 3 years for 30 x 30 sq km
And what will be new?

Single underground pipe for

- Telecom
- Grid Power in
- Water
- Sewerage
- Solar power out
- Cable TV
- Cooking gas
- Electric car charge
- Genset backup

Single window for all charges of municipal corporation
Transportation of cargo & freight thru mechanized tunnels
Ample lawns, waterways, and trees for each construction
Airport connects directly to

- city bus and interstate bus station
- local train and interstate mail
- car park, local cab and long-haul taxi

Cycle routes, walking paths, two-wheeler zones
History Museum, Olympic Stadium, Film city, Organic Farms
Space station for firing rockets into space and landing back
Planetarium with advanced telescopes for deep space Astro
Full-fledged University for 100,000 students

- Green Homes with solar roof tiles
- Green highway lighting with turbines and solar
- Electric cars, buses and trucks, bikes and autos
- Two large lakes with one a bird sanctuary
- Two mini dense forests with one for trekking
- A hill range for climbing and trekking
- A wildlife safari

A public temple without priests nor administration

If hearts could turn me
O if strings could pull me
& if friends could reach me

wish

I imagine a home with regular YOGA and HAVAN
I dream of a house with Satsang and Song
I wish to wake up at 4am and walk an hour
I fancy morning and evening Meditation
Weekly dance and music
Fortnightly badminton and tennis

And my fondest wish to sit at Guruji's feet

Sometimes you know

I feel good and free
Other times there is turbulence

At times my mind is silent and still
Then there are unending thoughts

sight

A great sight I beheld
There were divine sages and kings
There was laughter and soft chatter

Women passed by holding babies
Youngsters were playing in the park

Streetlights came on at sundown
Dusk bid adieu, night fell

Families ate a cozy dinner under lamplight

Is there something right and wrong?
Or is it all a matter of relative perception?

Is there anything forever wrong?
Is there anything always right irrespective of context?

If I am you and you are me
Who is OFF and who is ON?

toy

A rubber ball was the earliest toy
My grandfather played with me

I floated paper boats in rain made puddles
And felt like the Lord was close by my side

Birds woke me up from slumber
Their calls were shrill and sweet
When I stepped outside to greet
The sun waved as a cloud moved

sleep

Sleep is solace
Sleep is deep rest

Sleep makes me
Get up and go about my work
With a fresh heart and renewed
Confidence

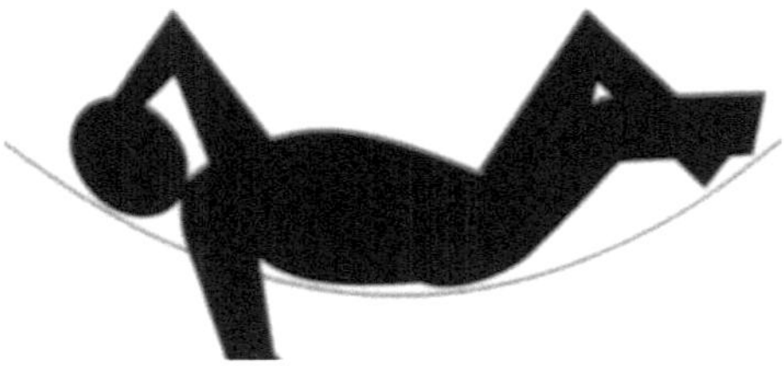

I yearn for the childhood joys
Marbles, skipping, staircase-climbing
Tricycle riding, fruit-plucking
Getting scolded, hiding and seeking

In my garden was a pair of butterflies
And a score of dragonflies

There were also some squirrels and frogs
Bulbuls, parrots, mynah and sparrows
Even few earthworms and snails

I know the challenges are stubborn
But my intellect is ready with sword

If I can resolve it in my head
There isn't any fear of loss

I could make my luggage vanish
Even my wallet was invisible till needed

The phone was a line in my palm
Then what for was any law or tax?

furniture

My room has many pieces of furniture,
There is a study desk and a book rack
There are wardrobes and a bed

But when I need to have a gathering
All them pieces become space
They make way for humans
                                        and free movement
They do not come in the way

S t r e t c h   your

W i d e n   your

Allow   the

i m a g i n a t i o n

horizon

Lord to enter in

Gates open when I wish
Locks shut without a wish

Lights glow soft and cream
Shadows slow down without support

river

The river called
I ran to it

The dolphins played
I raced with them

I remember riding a tonga to school
In my class X

Then I got a hero jet in my prep
And realized I could cycle
the entire town and not feel any fatigue

the Lord makes each so fit
and also lays guidelines so
          that one may never get old in the head
          nor
          have to beg for bread
          or
          steal for comfort
          and
sail happily to the next plane when time calls

young

some songs I hummed in the olden days
became forgotten

but whenever I was with friends
their talk tuned them back again
and I felt young

I was once a volcano
Then I became a turbulent cyclone

When it was time to frighten folks
I became thunder and lightning

But the children loved the show
The small ones hooted and sang

easy

It was easy to face the big corporates
It was child's play to bust the dictators

Soon I realized both were headless
So I patched them with cardboards

Bullets and bombs were no use
Poison and virus were ineffective

Schemes and plans made no sense
Strategy misfired and nothing held

Then it was discovered that I was
Not made of anything known to man

affection is in the moment
once past the flavor changes
and so does love and caring

though it surfaces again in a while
it is not the same emotion
the love's not so thick nor deep
but I guess it is just alright

strength wonders how come I am so strong
speed is tickled that I can easily beat it in a **race**

mystery

earth still has many a mystery

some forests few deserts none hath seen
many parts of the oceans are yet unknown
and many secretive companies and societies

but each man is also a mystery
his mind cells none hath unraveled
his heart none has touched bottom

my heart opens up to the innocent
can innocence be maintained?
can it be kept pure as snow?
only time will tell

death

death came easily and at the right hour
death erased my identity

it ensured i was removed from the history books, family albums, and government registers. It rubbed memories from peoples' heads, so that soon none knew me or of me. That was the complete rest. That was the long-term rest.

perhaps it couldn't reach deep inside the heart of someone who truly loved me. perhaps it considered that inviolable.

life is made up of expression.
there is also some intention.

only a life of attention is worth
it makes sense when you can

- have someone to share a joke or
- spend a quiet evening together
- do a group project
- participate in an event
- show that you belong and
- make Lord your own

heart

gold is the color of the heart
a heart is golden hued
my heart is made up of gold
it is malleable, ductile, soft and available

visit of the friend is a big thing
friend is rare to find and rarer to keep

friend is not family, so no strings are attached
friend lays no claim
friendships aren’t hereditary

tone your tongue
tone your attitude

tone down your presence
so nature fills you
and sets you free

clothes

buy your clothes and chappals
with your body in mind
even though society laughs
your body shall applaud

at times for a role
wear a foreign jacket
know it is temporary
and shuck it soon after

remember you are a traveler
for a limited timespan
soon you shall escape
and be free of conditions
and conditional notions

namah shivaya
namash shivaya
nama shivaya

based on your upbringing
and language
based on your perception
and role

you give the Lord your own name
he doesn't mind the spelling
he knows spellings are only for visa
or bank forms

and as a child you also know
whatever anyone calls you by
you gleefully respond and ack

names are valid for a lifetime
then they dissolve and fall

walking is divine
walks are integral
walk long or short
walk daily regularly

flowers

flowers also pray
that someone shall
kiss them
and make them
theirs

sap

herbs and bushes
shrubs and saplings
seeds and bulbs
or blades of grass

they seek a touch
they seek communion
they wish to chat
and share with

open your gates
open your windows

let the winds in
let breeze blow

sunlight raindrops
bits of space
and cosmic dust
make all yours
hug them all

school days or college times
let the children enjoy
let teens free to do their thing

don’t worry they won’t break
nor will they lose anything

they shall blossom forth
and make you proud
yes,
they shall make you smile

Be happy or sad
Be forlorn or mad
Be available
Be open to change
Be willing to listen

know

know that you are loved
know that you're precious
know that
know that deep inside

a visit to mercury
or to Venus is not a
farfetched idea

it just needs three
inventions

respiration chip
digestion bionic
movement pins

zoo

a zoo full of humans
a zoo made up of men
a zoo containing women

nah

such a zoo is rather flimsy
the inmates are never in
they are all about town
they need children to
keep them glued in

govern

better a city run by children
better a state governed by
the small boys and girls

why can't we do that?
try it out for a month
and see a better world

give them charge of a home
make them principal of a school

at least one university run by them

learning curves
or curvy figures

comics need readers
banks need workers
shops need stocks

scares are uncommon occurrences
they happen when one is least prepared
being frightened is not all that bad
re-remembering it may not be nice

scolding

a scolding is generally favored by mother
it is inbuilt in the mother-genes-code
even if you do not understand
it is destined to do some good

scoldings are scathing
scoldings are unbearable
scoldings prevent some unfavorable event
that is all one may think to apply as balm

headache is also terrible
but after it goes there is a calm
that calm is not otherwise experienced

escape

waiting to make a quick exit
by the right getaway chute

but where can one go?
having gone what can one do?
only after it happens may one know

so do not tarry
waste not a sec
take the high jump
when your turn comes

all may earn merit
few may earn wealth
merit unseen is better than seen wealth
merit alone brings a smile
tapas alone atones all error
debt-free is a life worth living
life is so beautiful when the soul is free

promise

best to make a promise
better still to break one
what is a promise if not kept
some promises need be shelved

breath is divine
or don’t you know
breath is heavenly
only when appreciated

see Him in the breath cloud on the mirror
how else would you acknowledge Him?

city

a city is built on hope
a city survives on commerce
a city needs trust
a city lives on culture
a city is where babies are born
a city is where we all say g'bye

a desktop is the first thing I remember buying
computers were my first love
I always thought I was an android
which they turned into a handheld
that filled my palm
and made me operable

a man-machine is not too distant
in-fact all machines are men at times
all men may be mechanical sometimes

someday we shall mingle with Strangers who are

- Emotions
- Thoughts
- Thoughtless
- Emotionless
- Bare body
- All-in-one
- Just space with a bare outline

memory

in my memory sits a memory
that was never there in the first place
the memory is named citta
it is fluid and stubborn both
and so's my life lived in stubborn and fluid pairs

discipline

i practice hard to maintain myself
discipline is a good friend
none better than self-discipline
in the list of friends

when I slept someone watched
when I watched someone slept
they say it was Heisenberg's
uncertainty principle
then why do I demand certainty
life is much better off without it

surprises some are so much welcome
more surprises and the mind cracks

sri krishna

I wished for a University
And I was granted the wish

I wished for a Spaceship
And companies raced to make them

I wished for Lord Sri Krishna
And he manifested alright

Someday my spaceship shall be designed
The ship which can accommodate a million
My ship has football fields, lakes, and schools
It can take off and land on water, air, or ground
It doesn't stuff stocks nor provisions
We simply produce in-house on need

the post office was my frequent destination
i felt I was writing to the divine and sending
Him things

Now I haven’t been there in a while
But the courier comes home frequently
It is all sent online and delivered in-house

to swim I didn't learn
to cycle I did
driving I cannot do
traveling a lot happens

I feel it in my gut
I shall move without transport
I shall travel not needing gadget

My bones are tensile
My feet are firm
My will can take me
across a world I own

many times I slipped
at times I blundered
nature forgave me
man too let it be

I feel I was brought up by the Gods
And felt surrounded by Celestials

Even when I travelled
The Lord sat beside me

Now I make it a point
To keep space for Him
I remember to keep my desk tidy
And my bed made up daily

He loves that, O Yes
He enjoys being pampered

my guru loves me no end
He always nudges my memory
tweaking my brain wo end

light

fires burning bright
flames shining bright
fireflies humming all night

their orange color is a sight
the dance moves are so right

blue are waters
waters are blue
pools are pretty
lakes are green

books I read
nay I hogged
it's been a while though
since I've opened one

do the mountains wish?
what do mountains desire?

perhaps a waterfall and a stream
maybe a path and a cave
the odd tiger and bear
and some loose stones

¿ ॠ 卐

μ √ ಉ

± ॐ Δ

∂ § [illegible]

[illegible] क◌ ∫

∑ œ ɸ

when words are insufficient
symbols suffice

emoticons are helpful
signs lead the way

ਲੁਧਿਆਣਾ ਜੰ.
लुधियाना जं.
LUDHIANA JN.

Move silently
Sit no shake
Speak softly
Sing with gusto

robot and science fiction
are truth not mere thought

as time goes by
anything you say
might come true
anything you wish for
might just be given to you

they say I was old
very very old, older than yonder tree
older than the city, older than gravity

if so there are parts of me
that are untouched by time and tide

I still have some ancient genes
that got made when the world was young
those will remain when civilizations fade
yes they shall be here even after I depart

they say I live on
through my sons and their sons

some say I live on
through my ideas and inventions

whatever it is
anyways said
makes me feel young
keeps me fresh and fit

21:31 bedtime

Epilogue

Once in a blue moon the magical Ships Sail, leaving a wake of exciting currents. If you are lucky, a bit of the magic falls on your countenance, & spins you out of the helpless orbit.

सर्वे भवन्तु सुखिनः । सर्वे सन्तु निरामयाः ।

सर्वे भद्राणि पश्यन्तु । मा कश्चिद् दुःख भाग्भवेत् ॥

ॐ शान्तिः शान्तिः शान्तिः ॥

When faith has blossomed in life,
Every step is led by the Divine.

Sri Sri Ravi Shankar

Om Namah Shivaya

जय गुरुदेव

www.ingramcontent.com/pod-product-compliance
Ingram Content Group UK Ltd.
Pitfield, Milton Keynes, MK11 3LW, UK
UKHW041348190726
13845UKWH00026B/481